Andy McNab became a so[...]
and joined the SAS in 19[...]
War he led the famous Bravo Two Zero patrol.
He left the SAS in 1993, and now lectures to
security and intelligence agencies in the USA
and the UK. He also works in the film industry,
advising Hollywood on training civilian actors
to act like soldiers, and he continues to be a
spokesperson and fundraiser for both military
and literacy charities.

Andy McNab has written about his life in the
army and the SAS in the bestsellers, *Bravo Two
Zero*, *Immediate Action* and *Seven Troop*. *Bravo
Two Zero* was made into a film starring Sean
Bean.

He is the author of over twenty bestselling
thrillers, several novels for children and three
previous Quick Read titles, *The Grey Man*, *Last
Night*, *Another Soldier* and *Today Everything
Changes*. With Dr Kevin Dutton he is the co-
author of *The Good Psychopath's Guide to Success*
and *Sorted! The Good Psychopath's Guide to Bossing
Your Life*. He has also edited *Spoken from the Front*,
a book of interviews with the British men and
women serving in Afghanistan.

www.andymcnab.co.uk
www.quickreads.org.uk

www.**transworld**books.co.uk

On the Rock

Andy McNab

CORGI BOOKS

TRANSWORLD PUBLISHERS
61–63 Uxbridge Road, London W5 5SA
www.transworldbooks.co.uk

Transworld is part of the Penguin Random House group of companies
whose addresses can be found at global.penguinrandomhouse.com

Penguin
Random House
UK

First published in Great Britain in 2016 by Corgi Books
an imprint of Transworld Publishers

A CIP catalogue record for this book
is available from the British Library.

ISBN
9780552172912
9780552172981 (export edition)

Typeset in 12/16pt Stone Serif by Falcon Oast Graphic Art Ltd.
Printed and bound by CPI Group (UK) Ltd, Croydon, CR0 4YY.

Penguin Random House is committed to a sustainable
future for our business, our readers and our planet. This book is made
from Forest Stewardship Council® certified paper.

MIX
Paper from
responsible sources
FSC® C018179

1 3 5 7 9 10 8 6 4 2

On the Rock

Chapter One

London: Friday, 4 March 2016, 11.36 a.m.

If you are called to a meeting at Vauxhall Cross, you know it means trouble. Vauxhall Cross is the home of what the press calls MI6 but is in fact the Secret Intelligence Service. People like me call it the Firm.

To the Firm I was a K. I had no idea what K stood for, but government departments like to make things more difficult than they really are.

I had to do the shit jobs that the government needed to be done, but was not allowed to do. If it was killing someone, stealing something, or just plain blackmail, the Ks did it. If the job went well then everyone was happy, apart from the bad guys. If it went wrong or the likes of me ended up in prison, the Firm said, 'Nothing to do with us, Guv.'

It was dangerous and no one would be coming to help me if I ever found myself deep in the shit. But I liked it. I liked having a letter instead of a name. I liked having no National Insurance number. I liked being paid in cash and paying no tax. I liked being in control of my own life. I did it because I was good at it and it was an easy way to pay for the things I wanted to do. I hadn't worked out what they were, though. I was a man with a lot on his mind but not too much in it.

I had not been called in by the Firm for nearly two years. Since then I had been getting up to stuff that could have got me into a lot of bother. And that was like gold dust to the Firm because they could use it to make you do what they wanted.

As I walked towards the offices from the tube station, the omens were not good. The March sky was dull, the River Thames seemed moody, and my path was blocked by roadworks. A burst from a drill sounded like the crack of a firing squad.

Vauxhall Cross is an odd-looking building on a miserable day. It looks like a beige and black pyramid that has had the top cut off, with large towers on each side and a bar looking over the river. If it had a few swirls of neon, it would look just like a casino. I missed the old building near Waterloo station. It might have been ugly, with loads of glass and lino tiles on the floor, but it was homely.

Opposite Vauxhall Cross, there was a raised

section of railway line, and beneath it grimy brick arches had been turned into shops. Two had been made into a massive motorbike shop. I was early for my meeting, so I popped in. Which bike was I going to buy to replace the one I had smashed up six months ago?

Okay, I admit it. I had been riding just a bit too fast on the M4 motorway. But it was two in the morning and I had had nothing better to do. Besides, I liked riding fast when I could get away with it.

It had started to rain and a big truck had been hammering along in the centre lane, throwing up a wet mist. I had moved out to overtake just as the driver had fallen asleep. The truck had swerved out of its lane and banged my left shoulder. The bike bounced across the road and smashed into the central barrier. I was thrown onto the other side of the motorway. Three sets of headlights were heading my way. I got up, closed my eyes and ran. I couldn't believe my luck as I scrambled onto the grass bank. I was so happy to be alive.

But my joy was short-lived. A few days later I got a bill for £1,228. I had to pay for the oil that had spilled on the road to be cleaned up and for my bike to be taken away.

I had decided not to get another bike.

Now, with the way my luck was going, I'd probably get killed some other way soon. Why not have a bit of fun while I could? I just couldn't decide between the red and the black Ducati. Not that it mattered much – it wasn't as if I was going to buy one.

I went into Vauxhall Cross through a metal door. Inside, it was like any office block in any city: very clean and sleek. People who worked there swiped a card through an electronic reader to get in but I had to go to the desk. Two women sat behind bomb-proof glass. I said to one, 'I'm here to see Mr Simmons.'

'Can you fill this in, please?' She passed a book through a slot under the glass, pointed to a camera and told me not to smile.

The book held tear-out labels. I wrote my name on one. It was put into a plastic holder for me to pin onto my jacket. My badge was blue and said, 'ESCORTED EVERYWHERE'.

The woman said, 'Somebody is coming down to pick you up. Take a seat.'

I sat on a long wooden bench that ran along the wall and waited. I was worried. There were only two types of meeting here for a low-life like me.

First there was the type with coffee and biscuits. It meant they were after you to do something that would get you into trouble. But at least you could choose to take the job or not. The second type of meeting had no coffee or biscuits. It meant you were in trouble and there would be pain. It didn't matter if you wanted to do the job or not.

A young man appeared. 'Good morning.'

I said, 'All right, mate?'

I liked to put on my London accent for the kids who had come into the Firm from university. One day they would be in charge and I wanted to let them know that people like me were not seen in those plush offices very often, but we were still part of the Firm.

He half smiled, led me into a glass bubble and locked me in. For a few seconds a machine sniffed and X-rayed me to make sure I had no bomb on me.

When the door opened again, he said, 'Come with me.' We went to a lift. He pressed the button and said, 'We're going to the fifth floor.'

The building was like a maze. I followed him. There was little noise coming from any of the offices but I could see people bent over papers or working on computers. At the far end of a corridor we turned into a room. There were smart wooden filing cabinets, and a couple of polished wooden tables had been pushed together to make a bigger work space.

The clerk took me to a closed door to one side of the large area and knocked on it. There was a crisp call from inside. 'Come!'

The young man turned the handle and ushered me in.

Chapter Two

Simmons was standing behind his desk. In his early forties, he was of average build, height and looks, but something marked him out as a high flyer. The only thing he didn't have, I was always pleased to note, was a lot of hair. I'd known him for about ten years and every time I had met him there was even less hair on the top of his head.

The one thing that had never changed in the past two years was the way Simmons dressed. He wore corduroy trousers, the colour of English mustard, and a shirt that looked as if he had slept in it. My eyes swept the room for coffee and biscuits. There were none.

At least Simmons had a smile on his face.

'Glad to see you,' he said. 'It has been a while. What have you been up to?' His voice held upper-class confidence, just like a judge's. He leaned over the desk and offered me his hand.

I shook it. 'This and that,' I said.

This was bad news. It was like the moment when your parachute has failed to open and you are just falling to earth. You have to accept the landing.

'Would you like a brew?'

That sounded better.

'Thanks. Coffee, white, no sugar.'

We sat down. I took a wooden chair on the other side of the desk. Simmons pressed his intercom and ordered the coffee. I had a quick look round the office for any clue about why I was there, but saw nothing.

His office looked over the Thames. It was a very plain room, apart from two Easter eggs on the window sill and a photo on the desk of a group I thought were his wife and two children. They all had hair. On the wall in one corner was a TV. The flat screen was showing news headlines from around the world.

His jacket hung on a coat-stand, and a squash bat, or whatever it was called, in a blue cover lay underneath it. It was as if a squash court was the unofficial meeting place for head spooks and the bat was the weapon of choice.

Simmons said, 'I've got a job that I want you to lead a team on.'

I looked at him. 'I work for myself now. You dumped me a couple of years ago.'

Simmons sat back in his leather chair and

smiled. 'No. I just put you in the freezer for a while.'

He handed me a photo of a couple, grinning, in matching red pullovers with a white pattern. They were sitting on a front-room carpet beside a large sheepdog. A picture of perfect bliss.

'Who are they?' I asked.

'Julie and Morgan Keen. They are American and are on a flight from Texas to Heathrow.'

I put the photo back on the desk. 'And I'm here because of these two?'

Simmons tapped the picture with a finger. 'Did you see the pullovers? This was taken two years ago when they were God-fearing Christians, doing good deeds.'

I checked out the photo again and saw that the white pattern on both of the pullovers was Santa on his sledge with lots of toys. Maybe it was the picture they had put on the front of their personal Christmas card.

'But soon after this photo was taken they became God-fearing Muslims,' Simmons added.

I knew that Islam was the fastest-growing religion in America, and many Christians had read the Koran to try to understand what that holy book said rather than believe what they read in the papers or heard on TV. Many liked what they read in the Koran and converted to Islam.

'You've got it wrong,' I said. 'God-*loving* Muslims, not God-fearing. Anyway, what are you saying? They may have converted but that doesn't make them terrorists.'

Chapter Three

There was a knock on the door. Two mugs of coffee arrived, but no biscuits. Maybe there were three types of meeting now.

Simmons picked up the plain white mug and I was left with the one that had a street sign for Albert Square. I didn't have Simmons down as an *EastEnders* fan but it was always good to learn new stuff.

Simmons took a sip of coffee as the clerk left the room. 'Of course it doesn't mean that they're terrorists. But the fact is, they have been groomed.'

I picked up my mug and drank some. It was horrible so I put it back on the tray. Simmons clearly agreed with me. His mug quickly followed.

'And that is what has happened,' he said. 'Julie and Morgan have been turned from true Islam by this man.'

He passed me another picture, this time of a man probably in his late twenties. He was coming out of a shiny steel and glass tower block. 'This is Demetri Alexander.'

The man's handsome face, neat brown hair and smart suit made him look like just the kind of guy any girl would want to take home to show off to her parents.

Simmons went on: 'He is a banker. He went to a private school and then to Oxford before he converted to Islam seven years ago. He then set himself up as an adviser to white British and American men and women who were thinking of doing the same thing. He called it "The Pathway to Allah".'

I put Alexander's picture on top of the photo of the Keens and gave the coffee another try.

'The only pathway he has is to a new kind of extremist group,' Simmons said, 'a white one.'

The coffee still tasted awful.

From the look on Simmons's face, I saw that this new type of terrorist was an immediate danger. I said, 'So Julie and Morgan are coming here to meet up with Alexander, then carry out an attack in London. Is that what you want me to stop?'

Simmons sat back in his chair, which squeaked as he pushed himself into it. 'Yes and no. They are coming here to meet Alexander but the attack is not to be in London. It is to take place in Gibraltar.' He handed me a folder. 'Something for you to read on the flight. You will meet the rest of your team on the Rock. Like you, they were in the SAS. You will know them all,' he said. 'There are thirteen pages. I want you to sign for them now and hand them over to the air crew when you've finished. Good luck.'

'Am I going now?' I asked. 'I don't have my passport with me.'

He said, 'Your passport is in the folder. Have you got your other documents in order?'

I was insulted. Passport, driving licence and credit cards are vital to any cover story. A K uses them to build up his or her cover: for example, they use the cards to buy things they need to make their story seem true. I had my cards with me, as always, but not my passport. The one Simmons handed me had probably been produced that morning.

The clerk came in and took me downstairs. I signed for the documents before I left; thirteen bits of paper with information on Alexander, his converts, and everything that Simmons knew about the attack, which wasn't much.

A car was waiting for me outside. I jumped into the front. When I was a kid, I'd look at people being driven around and they always sat in the back, not talking to the driver. I always get into the front and talk to the driver. That day my driver didn't want to talk, but I chatted to him anyway. It made me feel better about being driven around.

A helicopter was waiting at Battersea heliport, ready to take me to an RAF base for my flight to Gibraltar. Or, as Simmons had called it, the Rock. It sits at the bottom of Spain and is very small, but has a high mountain. It has been in British hands since some war Britain fought against Spain in the 1700s. The people there have UK passports and are as British as I am.

I had one last job to do before I boarded the helicopter. I called the family who would vouch for me if I was ever in a tricky spot. The Firm had put me in touch with them years ago. They were good people who wanted to help the country. If I got lifted by the police or anyone else, I could say, 'That's where I live – phone them, ask them.'

A man answered the phone.

'Jim,' I said, 'it's me. I've just been given a chance to go to Gibraltar with some mates. I might be there for a week. If it's more than that, I'll call again.'

Jim understood. 'The Browns next door had a break-in two days ago, and we're going to see Bob in Dorset over the Easter weekend.'

I needed to know those things. They were the sort of things I would know if I lived there all the time. Jim even sent me his local paper each week and I read it carefully. Now these details mattered even more than usual, because I had no idea what Simmons had in store for me.

Chapter Four

I was sitting outside a café in a square just off Main Street. It seemed that wherever I looked the mountain was sticking up above the roof-tops looking back at me.

I noticed that the lace on one of my trainers had come undone. I bent to do it up, and got a jab in the stomach from the magazine in my 9mm pistol.

I heard a loud hiss of air brakes and looked up to see a tour bus parking about twenty metres away. The sign on the windscreen said 'Young at Heart'.

The spring air was crisp under a bright blue Mediterranean sky, the morning sun just warm enough for me to wear only a shirt. The trees that lined the square were packed with birds so small I couldn't see them clearly among the branches, but they made enough noise to drown out the traffic.

I preferred to have my pistol stuck into my jeans at the front and centre of my body. The other three members of the team wore theirs on the side, but I had never got used to that. Once you find a position you like for your gun, you don't change. One day, you might try to pull it out and it isn't there – it's inches to the right. You're dead. Drawing a weapon is something that should never be thought about. All the thinking has to be about what made you reach for it in the first place. Just worry about whatever is in front of you and hope that you are quicker than the other person.

Senior citizens began to get off the bus. Marks & Spencer had made a fortune out of them. The men wore beige trousers, sensible shoes and V-neck pullovers over their shirts and ties. Most of the women were in polyester slacks with elastic waistbands and a sewn-in crease down the front. They all had tidy jet black or blue-rinsed hair. And they got very excited when they spotted the café and, as a herd, started to shuffle towards us.

The Young at Heart crowd were pleased at the promise of a pot of tea. We were already on our third pot while we waited for the bombers to turn up.

Even if they did appear, those thirteen sheets of paper Simmons had given me had not told us very much.

We thought the device would be a car bomb, but we didn't know what type of car or van it might be in. We didn't know which of the three bombers, whom we called players, was going to set it off. That would be the easy part for them: all it took was a mobile phone attached to the bomb, and all they had to do was call the mobile's number for the bomb to explode. If the player had the number on speed-dial, it would take just a couple of seconds.

But we didn't know for sure that the bomb would be in a vehicle. Perhaps it would be strapped to three suicide vests.

Maybe, maybe, maybe. Who knew what the players were planning? Only they did. But that was nothing new. We just had to get on with the information we had. All Simmons had been able to tell us was that a bomb attack would take place on the Rock today. It would happen during the Changing of the Guard at the Governor's Residence.

At 11 a.m. the soldiers of the Royal Gibraltar Regiment would be marching up Main Street in their red tunics and white helmets, behind their band, until they reached the square in front of the Governor's Residence. At 11.20 a.m., the Changing of the Guard would take place.

As usual, the square would be packed with

hundreds of soldiers and tourists. Families, lads on stag weekends and people on coach trips, like the Young at Heart lot, would line the route. When high explosives detonate, it's not just the blast that does the killing. Anything else that shatters – like glass, metal, concrete, even the victims' bones – becomes a small missile. It's as if hundreds of machine-guns had opened fire at the same time.

Many tourists would have selfie sticks to take pictures and videos of the Changing of the Guard. Some mobiles would survive the blast and their videos would show the world what had happened.

Our job was to capture the players alive so they could be questioned. We wanted to arrest them as they were trying to carry out their attack. We didn't want to arrest them after they had killed hundreds. That would mean a long court case, and by then any information we gained from them would be useless. They had to be caught in the act and grabbed. Then all three had to be made to tell us what they knew about this new terror group so that we could close it down.

Until we saw the players, the team – Naz, Slack Pat, Kev and I – were to stay where we were, drinking tea and reading the paper. We were waiting for something, somewhere, to happen.

Chapter Five

Through my radio earpiece I could hear Simmons. He was on board a Royal Navy warship at the Gibraltar docks. Everything he said was clear and calm.

'Hello, all call signs. This is Alpha. Radio check, over.'

Kev replied quietly into the microphone hidden under his shirt: 'Charlie.'

Slack Pat said, 'Delta.'

I heard Naz say: 'Echo.'

My turn came: 'Golf.'

Those were our call signs. They were quicker and clearer to use than names, especially when things got busy.

Once our team had finished the radio check, Simmons told us he had heard us all, which meant that the radios were working.

'Alpha.'

Naz always made me smile when he was talking seriously because he still sounded as if he should have been a market trader in the East End of London. Well, he did to me. His Arabic name meant 'delicate'. But, being the world's hairiest Pakistani man, he didn't look delicate. Especially as I had always had this vision of him in a pork-pie hat trying to sell dodgy perfume from his market stall.

The Young at Heart coach party settled down at nearby tables and picked up the menus. It was decision time for them – whether to have cake or go for soup and a sandwich. It was halfway between a mid-morning coffee and lunch time and they didn't know which way to jump.

I carried on looking bored, and that isn't easy. I had to look like I was really bored when I wasn't. If I didn't succeed, I would blow my cover. My team and I must not give away to any of the people around us what we were doing. That included the bombers. We all had to look like normal people while we were doing something else.

I had spent years being a Grey Man, blending in as best I could. No one ever gave me a second look. Years ago I worked undercover in Northern Ireland during the Troubles. I had been there about six months before I felt bedded in. By then, I *was* a local. I wore market jeans and cheap trainers. I needed to be moving about the city and be someone who wouldn't get a second look from anyone.

Wherever I went I had to fill my head with a reason to be there. If I found myself in a dangerous part of the city, I convinced myself I was going to see a mate. Even a mother walking her kids to school could be a danger to me. It takes less than a second for real people to sense something is wrong. That is especially true of young mothers so I always tried to avoid being near them. It must be something to do with their instinct to protect their child. Whatever it was, I knew that if I didn't get my act together a mother would be thinking, Who is he? Has he come from one of the estates on the other side of the river? Is he armed? Is he here to kill someone? Blow something up?

When someone notices you, things can go wrong.

Naz, Slack Pat and Kev all had the same background. Naz's experience wasn't in Northern Ireland where he would have stuck out like a sore thumb, just like I would have done in Baghdad. Today I was a tourist, having coffee with my mates. Just like the Young at Heart group, who had settled for soup and sandwiches.

Slack Pat leaned over and muttered into Kev's ear, 'New Jihad must be desperate. They've sent the Barry Manilow Fan Club. Is that your mum over there with them?' He grinned at Kev, who frowned.

Slack Pat was from Glasgow, with an accent to

prove it. Blond, blue-eyed, good-looking, clever and funny, he was everything I hated. He was also six foot two, and very fit. Pat's only saving grace, I thought, was that when he stood up there was nothing where his bottom should have been. He was called 'Slack' because he had lots of slack in the seat of his jeans.

I put my elbows on the table and leaned across it so I could keep my voice down. 'The file Simmons gave me said they call themselves New *Islamic* Jihad now.'

Slack Pat thought for a second, which was a long time for him, then shrugged.

Kev poured some more tea for Slack Pat. 'Thickhead.'

Kev's mother came from southern Spain, just a twenty-minute walk from where we were sitting on the Rock, and he looked like a local: olive skin, jet-black hair, about five foot ten but with the world's bluest eyes. His wife reckoned he looked like Mel Gibson, which he made fun of but secretly liked. He lived in a posh suburb with leafy streets and neat gardens. I wondered why Kev wanted a life like this.

It didn't matter to us what the bombers called themselves. All that did matter was that three of them were heading our way and we had to make sure they couldn't hurt anyone.

Chapter Six

The waiter smiled politely as the Young at Heart group gave him their orders slowly and loudly, just in case he didn't speak English.

'Can – I – have – the – soup – dear?'

Maybe they didn't know that on the Rock English is spoken everywhere and has been for hundreds of years.

They started taking pictures of themselves. Then they were swapping cameras so they could appear in their own photographs.

Slack Pat got up and said to them, 'Shall I take one of all of you?'

'Ooh, you're from Scotland, are you? Isn't it nice and warm now?'

He had just started doing his photo shoot when Simmons's voice filled our earpieces.

'Stand by, stand by. That's a possible, a possible . . . Bravo One on Main Street, heading south, towards the town square. Golf, acknowledge.' We had given the bombers the call sign 'Bravo' so everyone knew who we were talking about.

I got to my feet, confirmed to Simmons that I'd heard, and started walking. It was pointless all three of us moving at this stage. Simmons had probably seen someone who looked like one of our three targets on the Rock's CCTV cameras. He wanted me to go and see if it really was Bravo One – Alexander.

Families on their Sunday walks strolled across from my left. Tourists were taking pictures of buildings, looking at maps and scratching their heads; elderly locals were sitting down enjoying the weather, walking their dogs, playing with their grandchildren. There were two men with beer bellies, both old, smoking themselves to death. They wore trousers with big braces, shirt and vest to soak up the March sun. It was like any other day.

I wondered how many of them would survive if the bomb went off right there. I checked my watch. There was still an hour before the parade started for the Changing of the Guard.

I was just getting into my stride when Simmons was back on the radio. 'Stand by, stand by. That's a possible Bravo Two and Bravo Three on Main Street heading north towards the Town Square. Charlie, confirm.'

Kev got on his radio. 'Roger that.'

His task was the same as mine, to confirm that the possible Bravo Two was Morgan and Bravo Three was Julie.

I imagined Kev walking along the pavement like me, looking in shop windows and doing the normal lazy Sunday thing, blending into the crowd as he checked out the possibles.

I hit Main Street and saw Bravo One straight away. He wore a brown pin-striped suit jacket – he'd had it for so long that the pockets sagged. The back was creased because he'd been wearing it in a car. His jeans were old and faded. He didn't look like a slick banker today but, of course, he didn't want to. It was definitely him.

I got on the radio. 'Alpha, this is Golf. That's confirmed. Bravo One, brown pin-stripe on faded blue.'

Then Naz was on the radio. 'Echo is now backing you up, Golf.'

Naz was short, with an acne-scarred face. He had the world's biggest motorbike back home. I liked to tease him because when he sat on his bike he couldn't get both feet to touch the ground at the same time. I looked on him as a brother. Naz and I had been young soldiers together and had got into the SAS at the same time. We'd been best friends ever since. He was always calm. I'd been with him when the police arrived to tell him that his sister had been murdered. He just said, 'I'd better go to London and sort things out.' Of course he cared but he didn't get excited about anything. I always felt secure when he was backing me up.

As I followed Alexander, I informed everyone that Bravo One – Alexander – was still moving south on Main Street. Then he turned into the square by the Governor's Residence.

There were six or seven cars parked in the shade, against the wall of an old building. I saw Alexander push his hand into his jacket pocket as he went towards them. Was he about to set off a bomb?

Without slowing his stride, he focused on one vehicle and headed towards it. I moved so I had a clear view of the number plate.

'Alpha, this is Golf.' I read out the car's number.

I pictured Simmons with the computers in front of him in the control room. He confirmed that he'd heard me. 'Roger that. The car is a white Ford Focus. '

'It's on the right, third car from the entrance,' I said.

By now the keys were in Alexander's hands.

'Bravo One at the car, he's at the car.'

I had to pass him quite close now – I couldn't change direction. I could see his profile. His chin and top lip were covered with zits, and I knew what that meant. He had been suffering from stress.

Alexander was still at the Ford. He turned, now with his back to me, pretending to sort his keys out, but I knew he was checking the tell-tales: maybe a sliver of Sellotape across a door, things arranged in a certain way inside the vehicle. If they were not as he had left them, Alexander would run.

By now, Naz would be near the entrance to the square, ready to 'back'. If I was too exposed to the target, he would take over, or if I got into trouble and weapons came out, Naz would help me to finish it.

The buildings were casting shadows across the square. I couldn't feel any breeze, just the change in temperature as I moved out of the sunlight.

I was too close to Alexander now to transmit on my radio. As I walked past the car I heard the click of the lock as Alexander pressed the key fob.

I headed for a wooden bench on the far side of the square and sat down as Simmons spoke again over the radio. 'This is Alpha. The car was rented at Malaga airport two days ago by Morgan.'

They must have driven from the airport, crossed the border and parked it straight away to make sure the device would be in place.

Alexander made a sudden movement, and I

got back on the radio: 'Alpha, this is Golf. His feet are on the ground, but he's fiddling under the dashboard. Wait.' Could he be making the final connections to the bomb?

As I was speaking without moving my lips, an old man came towards me, pushing his bike. He was on his way over for a chat. I didn't want to discuss local politics or the weather, but I didn't want to annoy him because he might somehow draw Alexander's attention.

The old boy stopped, one hand on his bike, the other swinging around. He asked me a question. I didn't understand what he had said – he had spoken in Spanish. I smiled and shrugged. I'd done the wrong thing: he said something that sounded angry, then wheeled his bike away, arm still swinging.

I got back on the radio. I couldn't see exactly what Alexander was doing, but both of his feet were still outside the car. He was sitting on the driver's seat and was still leaning under the dash. It looked as if he was trying to get something out of the glove compartment – as if he'd forgotten something and gone back to get it. I couldn't confirm what he was doing but his hands kept going into his pockets.

Everything was closing in. I felt like a boxer – I could hear the crowd, I was listening to the referee, listening for the bell, but mostly I was focused on the man I was fighting. Nothing else mattered. Nothing. The only important people in the world were me and Bravo One.

Then, through my earpiece, Kev broke into my world: 'Alpha, this is Charlie. That's confirmed – Bravo Two and Three. Both of them are still heading north on Main Street towards the square. They have suitcases.'

They were coming towards us.

Chapter Seven

Slack Pat was on the radio: 'Delta's backing Charlie.'

He was the last of the team to move from the café: he had to support Kev.

Kev came back on the radio. 'Bravo Two and Three are still heading towards the square.'

Simmons cut in to make sure we knew what to do. 'All call signs, I still do not have control. Let them meet. There is still time before the Changing of the Guard.'

Simmons hadn't got control. That meant he hadn't received the final order to carry out the job. He had only one boss and that was the Prime Minister. It was never talked about but all four of us in my team were aware that the Prime Minister had to give the final order for Simmons to carry out the arrest.

The reason was simple. If it went wrong, a lot of lives would be lost, and the Gibraltar government would be angry that such a dangerous operation had taken place without their knowledge.

That was why we, the Ks, were on this job.

I recognized the other two players as soon as they turned the corner and walked into the square.

Bravo Two was Morgan. He was a butcher by trade and, with his round face and red cheeks, he looked as if he had eaten too many meat pies.

Julie, who was Bravo Three, was smaller and, like her husband, loved those pies. An ex-convent schoolgirl, with black curly hair past her shoulders, she looked angelic.

Both wore the same hooded jacket and jeans with nice clean white trainers. Julie had even given herself the American tourist look: she had a camera dangling from her neck and a street map in her hand.

But it was the large wheelie suitcases that worried me. They were brand new and, from the way they dragged them over the square, they were heavy.

I wanted to get this over and done with before anything could go wrong. But instead I had to watch as the two men shook hands by the Focus and Julie looked on as a dutiful wife. Then she opened the car's boot.

I kept talking on the radio, explaining to everyone what was happening as the two men placed the heavy suitcases in the boot. Then the Keens stood in front of Alexander, hiding him as he bent into the rear of the car and stayed there far too long. I watched as he closed the boot and the three bombers started to talk. Julie leaned back against the car, the two men standing and facing her. If I hadn't known differently, I would have thought they were trying to chat her up.

Then Julie gave Alexander her camera, and Morgan stood at the rear of the Focus with her. They played the happy couple while Alexander got the camera on them.

But he wasn't taking pictures – it was video. I couldn't hear what they were saying but their faces showed no sign of stress. Now and then I heard laughter above the traffic noise as they spoke into the lens. They were pointing into the square and then to the car. Once they had stopped filming, Alexander got out a packet of mints and passed them round. Then he took the memory card out of the camera and placed it in his jeans pocket. He opened the boot once more and threw in the camera.

To me and the rest of the team dotted about the square that meant only one thing. Alexander had checked that the bombs in the suitcases were ready to explode when he made the call from his mobile. All they were waiting for now was the Changing of the Guard.

But what about the video?

That was the Keens' suicide video and would be shown online after the explosion. Maybe they were going to stay in the square and detonate the device so the attack happened when it could do the most damage.

Simmons was back on the radio. 'Hello, all call signs, all call signs. I have control. I have control.'

Great. Now it was down to me and the rest of the team. Like dogs, we had been let off our leads and no one could tell us what to do. Not Simmons, not even the Prime Minister. That was because we were the people on the ground. No one else would be seeing, hearing or even smelling what we would. Only we could make decisions on what to do when the bombers were in our hands.

Chapter Eight

Simmons had picked us for the job because once we were let loose we knew what we were doing.

The Focus's lights flashed as Alexander locked the car, and the bombers started to walk away. I spoke on the radio: 'Stand by, stand by. That's all three Bravos now moving away from the car, back towards Main Street.'

I went on: 'All call signs. Let them pass and we'll follow until I think it's safe to lift them.'

I was glad they weren't going to stay in the square with the car because there were far too many people around for us to take the bombers safely. For all I knew, they were armed and wanted to go out in a blaze of glory when they tried to set off the device.

Things went well as the team let the players pass. We followed them on Main Street and turned left, going the same way Alexander had come. They were all looking very happy as they chatted away and played at being tourists. This was good because we were heading towards the airport and the border crossing. The further north we moved the better: there was more open space and fewer people were about.

Maybe the players were not going to stay on the Rock to set off the bomb. Maybe the plan was to detonate it from Spain at 11.20 a.m. when the soldiers and onlookers would be in the square.

It didn't matter what their plan was. I would take them well before that bomb exploded.

Simmons was back on the radio: 'Hello, all call signs, all call signs. Cancel, cancel, cancel! I do not have control! Cancel! Golf, acknowledge.'

I made a much less formal reply: 'What the hell's going on? Tell me – what's going on?'

'Wait . . . wait . . .' Simmons was tense. I had never heard that in him before. There were voices in the background and he had to shout for me and the team to hear him. 'All stations, all stations, I need another ID. I need to be one hundred per cent sure. Golf, acknowledge.'

The Prime Minister must have been flapping. No wonder they wanted the likes of us on this job. If it went wrong there would be hell to pay.

'Roger that, Alpha,' I said. 'But I can confirm that we have Bravo One, Two and Three.'

On board the ship, it sounded like a chimps' tea party. Radio networks back to the UK would be full of chatter as the Prime Minister asked more questions. He wasn't sure if he should hand over control once more.

Simmons came back: 'I need you to check again. I've sent someone to check the vehicle.'

A bomb disposal guy was on the Royal Navy warship, ready to check out the device. He was on his way to do just that. Now the Prime Minister also wanted to know if there really was a device in the Focus. This was turning into a farce and all we could do was follow the bombers and wait.

I got back on the radio. 'Bravo One, Two and Three are leaving Main Street and heading towards the airport and border. Tell the bomb disposal guy to hurry up. Checking them again now.'

Chapter Nine

I was now on the other side of the road and wanted to get in line with them so that I could see their faces again.

'Alpha, this is Golf. I confirm we have Bravo One, Two and Three. One hundred per cent. Over.'

There was more chatter on the radio. Simmons was still tense. Telephones were ringing and people were milling about.

'Roger that, Golf. I still do not have control. The car has the explosives on-board. The device is live. The bomb disposal expert is trying to disarm it but it will take time. Wait.'

I cut in on the radio, without answering Simmons: 'All call signs, let's keep on top of them until someone somewhere makes a decision.'

The three bombers were still chatting as Alexander handed out more mints. They continued to stroll along the street.

Checking behind me, I saw Naz on the other side of the road, backing me up. His eyes were focused on the bombers. Kev and Slack Pat would be keeping out of their sight and moving up the side roads, trying to get ahead of them. That way we would have them boxed in. If they checked behind them, Naz and I would pull back and let the other two follow. Then we would get into the side streets and out of sight.

But for now our targets were not worried about being followed. They chatted away as they headed towards the airport and border crossing.

'Alpha, this is Golf. They are now on Churchill Avenue and still heading north. You need to get your finger out. I have to take them now.'

Simmons knew the danger. We still had a live device and only we could stop the bombers detonating it.

'Golf, you must wait, wait . . .'

I could still hear noise in the background: lots of talking, more phones ringing, people shouting instructions.

Then everything went quiet on the ship, apart from Simmons. He was still hoping for the same thing as I was. 'Wait . . . wait . . .'

I hoped it was the Prime Minister on the other radio.

All I could hear now was my pulse pounding in my head. Then, at last, the voice of Simmons – very clear.

'All call signs, this is Alpha. I have control. I have control. Golf, acknowledge.'

I got back on the radio: 'All call signs, all call signs, if they get as far as the runway, we'll have them there. If not – on my word, on my word. Stand by.'

The airport runway cut across the Rock. If you were walking or driving to the airport or to the border you had to cross the runway. It was the safest place to take the three because it was a wide-open space and there were few people about.

But then the three bombers reached a junction just ahead of me.

'Stop, stop, stop!' I said. 'That's all three now at the crossroads. Charlie and Delta, come out onto the road. As soon as I see you, we will lift them. Remember, the device is live. They must not detonate it.'

I didn't know why they were stopping and didn't care. Now had to be the time to take them – just in case they were about to split up.

I waited in a doorway as the three players stood at the crossroads. Alexander was doing the talking while the other two nodded. They weren't just chatting. Alexander was giving instructions. I checked behind me. Naz was letting a mother and a wheelchair pass him as he moved up the avenue to get level with me. As soon as Kev and Slack Pat had the other side of the junction covered we would move in.

But then the three split up. Alexander left the other two and crossed the road, still walking towards the airport. The Keens turned right. They must be heading back towards the square.

Chapter Ten

I had to split the team. We had to take all three bombers at the same time so no one had the chance to detonate the device.

'Charlie and Delta, let Bravo One pass you, then stay with him. When you're ready to lift him, me and Echo will take the other two.'

I moved out of the doorway and got to the crossroads at the same time as Naz did to see the Keens walking along hand in hand, with Julie nearest the road.

Simmons wanted to know what was happening.

Now wasn't the time for me to tell him. It was time for Simmons to shut up. I needed to stick to the Keens, with Naz now close by, just waiting for Kev to get on his radio and tell me that he and Pat were ready. Anyway, it wasn't Simmons who needed to know what was going on. He would never ask for information when the team were at their most dangerous point in a job. Maybe the Prime Minister was flapping again.

'Wait out,' I said

I kept my eyes on the Keens as cars passed and

families came out of shops with the Sunday papers under their arms, their kids eating ice cream. None of them knew what was about to happen between the nice American couple and the two men behind them. But they soon would.

Just then, I heard a police siren in the distance, followed by gunfire.

At the same instant Kev came on the radio: 'Contact! Contact!'

More shots.

Naz and I looked at each other. What was going on?

The Keens had also heard the siren and the shots. They turned back towards us. We were five metres away from each other and Julie's eyes were as big as plates. She was searching frantically for the source of the noise.

A woman came out of a shop just to our right and got between us. Naz shouted at her, 'Down! Down!' With his left hand, he pushed her to the side. She banged into the shop window and fell over, blood pouring from her head. At least she wouldn't get up and become a target.

She was screaming, which made all the people in the area start to scream.

The Keens knew the game was up but they were not defeated yet. Both stood where they were, looked at each other and prepared to die together as their hands went towards their jacket pockets.

From the corner of my eye I saw Naz flick back his jacket to reach into his holster. But I wasn't really looking at him. I was looking at Julie's hand moving to the right side of her jacket. She and Morgan weren't morons. The moment they had heard the gunfire and seen us, they had known the score.

Julie and I had eye-to-eye. She knew what I was going to do. She could have stopped going for her pocket. She could have put her hands up.

My jacket was held together with Velcro so that I could pull it apart and draw my pistol.

The process of drawing and using a weapon takes place in stages. The slower it felt, the faster I knew it would be. It took me less than a second.

Stage one: With my left hand I grabbed a fistful of jacket and pulled it hard towards my chest. The Velcro ripped apart. I was sucking in my stomach and sticking out my chest to make the pistol grip easy to grab. You only get one chance.

We still had eye contact. Julie was shouting but I couldn't hear her.

55

Stage two: I pushed my right hand onto the pistol grip – if I got this wrong I wouldn't be able to aim correctly. My lower three fingers grasped it. My index finger was outside the trigger guard, parallel with the barrel – I didn't want to pull the trigger early and kill myself. Julie was still shouting, her hair flying around her head as she flicked it from side to side. I was still focused on her head but could see that her hand was coming out of her jacket pocket. I didn't know what was in her hand, but that didn't matter. We had made our decisions.

Stage three: I drew my weapon, taking the safety catch off with my thumb. Our eyes locked again as she stopped moving her head. Julie knew she had lost the race and stopped shouting. Her lips curled. She was going to die.

As my pistol came out, I flicked it parallel with the ground. No time to extend my arms and get into a stable firing position.

Stage four: my left hand was still pulling my jacket out of the way and the pistol was now by my belt buckle. There was no need to look at it. I knew where it was and what it was pointing at. I kept my eyes on Julie and hers never left mine. I pulled the trigger.

The report seemed to bring everything back into real time. The first round hit her. I didn't know where – I didn't need to. As she hit the ground she rolled and I could no longer see her hands.

I kept firing as I brought the weapon up into the correct aim and moved forwards, Naz was doing the same with Morgan. There is no such thing as overkill. If they could still move, they could detonate the bomb. If it took a whole magazine of bullets for me to be sure I'd stopped Julie setting off that car bomb, I would fire it. She was curled up in a ball, holding her stomach. I moved forwards and fired two aimed shots at her head. She was no longer a threat.

We ran the last couple of steps to the bodies as people screamed, hid in doorways, lay in the road and ran everywhere.

I grabbed Julie's shoulder and pulled her over. As she turned, a mobile fell from her hand. I picked it up as Simmons shouted into my earpiece: 'I need you to report to me. Over!'

Naz had Morgan's mobile in one hand. As he wiped the blood off his hands onto Morgan's jeans, he pointed down an alleyway. 'We need to get out of here.'

We holstered our weapons and ran, turning corners into narrow alleyways, trying to avoid dustbins and mopeds until we were far enough from the screams.

Gulping air, we ripped open the backs of the phones and took out the batteries as Simmons yelled into our earpieces.

I spoke to him. 'Alpha, this is Golf. Bravo Two and Bravo Three are dead. They were going for their mobiles to detonate.'

Kev got onto his radio. He and Pat were in some other hiding place, doing the same as we were. 'This is Charlie. Bravo One is dead. I have his mobile and the memory card. Bravo One thought the siren was for him. When we had eye contact he knew what was going to happen. He went for his mobile. The police – what happened with the siren?'

We began to walk along the alleyways towards the docks.

Simmons explained, 'It was just a normal 999 call, nothing to do with us. The expert is still disarming the device. We stopped the attack. Well done. But now they are dead we have lost a way of finding out more about their group. The other members will probably go to ground now. We won't find them.'

I got on the radio. 'This is Golf. I have an idea.'

Naz and I came out of an alleyway into a street. People were rushing about and more police sirens filled the air. Blending in with the real people once more, we headed towards the Royal Navy warship.

Naz stopped. 'Listen . . . Can you hear that?'

I could just about hear the band playing as they marched up Main Street with the new guard.

Chapter Eleven

East London: 8 April 2016, 7.29 p.m.

I sat with Naz over egg and chips in a café. The news was being shown on the world's biggest flat-screen TV high above the till. It had been over a month and still there appeared to be nothing to report but the shootings on the Rock. They weren't even discussing the bomb that had been disarmed.

Naz started to make a chip sandwich with the two slices of bread and butter that had come with the heart attack on a plate. 'You know what? If any more armchair experts tell us what happened and why, I might start believing them!'

I nodded and covered my chips with tomato sauce as we listened to another one telling the world what had happened as if they had been there. But none of them knew what they were talking about. The truth was far simpler.

The Keens had made their suicide video by the car, and Alexander had taken the memory card from the camera. They had then started to walk back towards the border crossing. The three had parted at the junction. Julie and Morgan were going back to the square to be part of the crowd during the Changing of the Guard. It was just as I had thought. They had wanted to detonate the car bomb when it would cause the most damage, the most deaths. Both of them had mobiles in their jacket pockets with just one number on speed-dial. It belonged to the mobile phone attached to the bomb.

Maybe they had planned to scream their loyalty to New Islamic Jihad before blowing themselves up. Maybe they hoped a surviving camera or mobile would capture their message. Who knows? Who cares? All that mattered was that they never got the chance.

As for Alexander, he hadn't planned to blow himself up. He was heading back to the border with the memory card that held the Keens' video. By the time the bomb went off, he would have walked across the border into Spain. He would have used his mobile to dial up the bomb at the end of the Changing of the Guard in case the Keens had bottled it.

All he would have had to do then was post the video online after the bomb had gone off and the shit would have hit the fan. He would have got a flight back to the UK, and gone back to work in the City. Then he would have started looking for others to blow themselves up.

But when he had seen Slack Pat and Kev, as the police siren kicked off, he had had no choice but to go for his mobile and try to detonate, just as the Keens had.

Naz and I could only smile as another reporter interviewed the Keens' next-door neighbour. She couldn't understand what the couple had done. After all they were white, American and God-fearing. Perhaps the devil had taken their souls. She'd have a priest come to her house in case the devil had jumped over the fence to take her soul too.

In the London studio, a human-rights lawyer was saying that the level of violence used against the terrorists had been far too high.

Naz was worked up now. 'How can you over-shoot a terrorist?'

The lawyer was going to sue whoever was responsible for the killings. Just as soon as he had discovered who had carried them out.

Naz was finishing off his last egg by dipping his chip sandwich into the yolk as I pointed my fork at the screen. 'That's the trouble with twenty-four-hour news,' I said. 'They just have to fill the air with junk.'

Naz nodded as he wiped egg off his chin.

Then he looked out of the large window to the street. He checked his watch and took a gulp of tea. 'Mate, it's nearly time,' he said. 'If you're late Simmons won't be happy. After all, it was your idea.'

I finished off my chips, ramming the last few into my mouth to chew on the way. We went out into the street to join the others heading towards the mosque. The last of the day's five prayers was about to start and we didn't want to miss it.

Naz had been taking me to his mosque because I wanted to learn more about Islam. Who better to teach me than a Muslim?

The call to prayer sounded out across the roof-tops as we walked through the wrought-iron gates of what had been an old warehouse, past men and women in their queues for the mosque's washrooms. Little kids ran in and out of the legs of middle-aged men in business suits. Teenagers stood around chatting to grannies. Naz and I mingled with the crowd, smiling at everyone as they waited to clean themselves in preparation for prayer.

Quite a few guys were already on mats outside the mosque. They were getting their prayers in early. Maybe they had to be back at work or babysitting.

I stayed with Naz as we dumped our shoes on the shelves at the entrance. The routine was always the same: hands, mouth, nose, face, fore-arms, wet hands over head to the back of the neck, then ears. Once you had done your feet, you were ready to roll. Naz had brought a pair of flip-flops with him so he didn't have to put his socks back on.

Non-Muslims are welcome in mosques. They don't like you trying to take part if you're not one of the faithful, but you can stand at the back and watch – it's no big deal. Word had spread in this mosque that I was thinking of converting, and I was made very welcome.

From where I was standing at the entrance to the washroom, I had a clear view of the road and could see a man in a dark grey suit outside the iron gates.

Naz had finished cleaning himself and was hopping over to me, trying to get his other flip-flop onto his foot. He, too, had seen the man outside the gate. 'Mate, that has got to be him.'

I turned towards the door. 'I'm about to find out. See you tomorrow.'

I left Naz to his prayers and walked against the flow of people heading for the mosque. As the man turned towards me, I reached the gates and held out my hand. He took it but didn't say a word. It was up to me to say the greeting first. Some Muslims believe they shouldn't be the first to say, 'Peace be upon you,' to a non-Muslim. He looked the formal type – or maybe he was just testing me.

He shook my hand when he heard the greeting and gave me a sparkling smile. 'And peace be upon you also,' he replied.

'You must be James Bowden,' I said.

He kept up the smile. 'Yes, that's me.' The smile stayed as he pretended to tighten his tie. 'Not quite what you expected?'

I looked him up and down as if I was checking out a used car. He was well dressed, with bright blue eyes to match his tie. He should have been hosting an American game show, apart from his very posh British accent. 'No, not at all,' I lied. James was exactly what I'd expected. He had replaced Alexander.

James finished with his tie. 'Well, that's the problem with emails. No personal contact. By the way my Islamic name is Haddi. It means "I am a guide".'

I nodded. 'Nice to meet you in person, Haddi. The name suits you. It explains what you do for the Pathway to Allah.'

We started to walk.

'Once I had converted, I really wanted to help

others do the same,' he said. 'That's why I chose the name . . . So, why do you want to become a Muslim?'

I shrugged as we crossed the road at the traffic lights. 'A couple of years ago, I was reading about Islam. I didn't trust what I was seeing in the media and just wanted to learn what it was really about.'

Haddi nodded as I told him the story he must have heard a thousand times before. 'So, the more you read, the more you understood?'

Now it was my turn for the big smile but I wasn't giving away what I was thinking, and neither was Haddi. 'Exactly,' I agreed.

'People really don't understand people like us who have taken a different path. They feel confused and that makes them scared. But that's all right. You have no control over what they think, only over what you believe.'

I nodded, looking like I was thinking hard about what Haddi had said. In fact I was waiting for him to fill the gap.

He did so. 'How does that make you feel? You know, people not understanding why you want to convert.'

I had him where I wanted him. 'I feel angry that I am already thought of as low-life, second class, maybe even a terrorist.'

Haddi nodded in silent agreement as we passed the café. The news was still on, showing clips from Gibraltar before cutting back to the studio. There, two middle-aged women sat at either side of the male presenter. The banners below them told us they were both eye witnesses to the shootings.

Haddi stopped and looked into the window. 'What do you think about those three bombers? After all, they were converts.'

I stood next to him and watched the TV. The two women were obviously arguing about whose version of events was correct. 'I think what they were trying to do was wrong.' I turned to face Haddi so that he could read my eyes as well as hear my words. 'But you know what? I understand why they wanted to do it. I understand their anger.'

The women were angry with one another now. We watched them for a few more seconds before we walked on.

Haddi wasn't smiling now but in deep thinking mode. 'Yes, I agree with you. I too understand their anger.'

He stopped outside a branch of Greggs and pulled an expensive leather wallet from inside his jacket. 'Here.' He handed me his business card. 'Why not come to one of our meetings tomorrow night? The Pathway to Allah will be very happy to guide you along your journey to Islam.'

I took the card, and Haddi carried on with his sales pitch. 'In your emails, you said you had a friend in the mosque. Don't forget that some people there will still be suspicious of you.'

I put the card into my back pocket.

Haddi had got into his stride now. 'The Pathway to Allah is all about people like us converting to Islam. We understand the problems and we understand your fears because we have all been there ourselves.' He placed his hands on my shoulders. 'Will you come?'

'Yes.'

Haddi was very happy. 'Excellent! I know the perfect Islamic name for you. You shall become Abdul Azeem, "Servant of the Almighty". Sounds good, doesn't it?' He turned back the way we had come.

I went down a side road towards my brand-new Ducati Monster, which was standing next to Naz's dirty BMW GS. My new bike was red and shiny, with my shiny new helmet locked onto the seat.

I pulled out a cheap pay-as-you-go mobile and hit speed-dial. It rang twice before Simmons answered from his desk at Vauxhall Cross. 'Well?'

'I'm in. My first meeting is tomorrow night and it shouldn't be long before I'll be asked to join New Islamic Jihad instead of becoming a law-abiding Muslim at Naz's mosque for wimps.'

I knew Simmons wanted to go home. Perhaps he had had a long day.

'Your idea has worked so far,' he said. 'Well done.' He cut the call.

I threw the phone into a builder's skip. Then I unlocked my helmet, kicked the bike into first gear and rode off down the street.

Game on.

If you've enjoyed this Quick Read title,
why not try another Andy McNab book?

Keep reading for an extract from

RED NOTICE

Prologue

Borjomi, Georgia

25 September 1996
05.17 hrs

Dawn had begun to streak the eastern sky as the two mud-spattered trucks inched their way up the road in the faint glow from their sidelights. They jolted over rain-filled potholes and scree and came to a halt just short of the crest of the hill.

Their movements measured and cautious, a dozen armed men climbed down from the rear of each vehicle. Their breath billowed around them in the freezing air. Checking their safety catches, they stamped their feet to restore circulation and eased the stiffness from their legs. Some placed a last cigarette in the middle of their week-old beards and lit up.

They checked their equipment, ensuring pouches were still secure. If it had a button or a Velcro strip, it was there to be fastened. Two of the team struggled to hoist heavy weapons systems onto their shoulders.

Their commander stood a short distance apart from his men. Laszlo had an aversion to the smell of nicotine. He wore the same stained camouflage fatigues as his troops and had a similarly Slavic cast to his features, complete with coarse, almost black beard, but carried himself with an arrogance they didn't share. He was just short of six feet in height, but his sinuous limbs and slim frame made him look taller. His mouth was downturned and his eyes were the washed-out grey-blue of a winter sky; his skin was so pale he looked as if he'd lived his life in permanent shadow.

Another man exited the cab of the nearest truck. Laszlo's cool gaze missed nothing as he approached. The newcomer's civilian clothes were of a cut and quality that were neither cheap nor local. He wasn't a Slav, he was from the West. Europe? The USA? It was hard to tell. They all looked the same. His brown hair was starting to grow out from its short back and sides, and he, too, had a good week's growth on his chiselled jaw.

The man might not have been one of Laszlo's team, but the comfortable way he held his AK, the folding butt closed down in his hand as if it were a natural extension of his body, showed that he was no stranger to shot and shell. The weapon – all of his equipment – was also of Soviet origin. In Yeltsin's Russia, there was no shortage of underworld gangs willing to steal and trade such things, or of corrupt officers happy to empty their armouries in return for cold, hard cash.

The man had no fear of repercussion from what he was about to do. There would be nothing to suggest this had been anything but a purely local affair. He was sterile of ID and personal documentation. Like the rest of the team, it was as if he didn't exist. He had a name – Marcus – but Laszlo knew it wasn't his own. The team commander had taken steps to discover his companion's real identity. Information was a commodity to be traded, like drugs, weapons and women, and Laszlo always liked to bargain from a position of strength.

He stood for a couple more minutes, watching the new day creep across the landscape. To his right, a steep, boulder-strewn slope tumbled to a fast-flowing river. Water the colour of chocolate surged downstream. The force of the current had carved out the soil for a ten-metre stretch along the far bank, exposing a latticework of tree-roots that gleamed white against the mud, like the ribs of a putrefying corpse.

On the other side of the road, a dense pine forest cloaked the lower slopes of the mountains that filled the northern horizon. It seemed to float in a sea of mist. The treetops swayed each time there was a gust of wind. As he watched, the sun's first rays painted the snow-capped peaks with gold. In the west, just visible now in the strengthening light, a black gash as straight as a Roman road showed the course of the pipe-line being driven through this remote valley. Directly in its path, just over the hill from where they now stood, a huddle of buildings lay surrounded by a patchwork of fields.

As soon as the man reached him, Laszlo turned. The wind whipped up a shower of pine needles as the two of them moved through the edge of the forest. As they neared the crest of the hill, they flattened themselves to the earth and wormed their way to a point from which they could study the approach to Borjomi.

On the slope below, the trees gave way to fields of yellowing grass, dusted with frost and punctuated by mounds of autumn hay secured beneath tarpaulins. Beyond them, houses were clustered around a dusty square. A rusting iron water pump and a long stone horse-trough stood at its centre, half shaded by a large, stag-headed oak tree.

The buildings at the heart of the village were of wood and stone, with sun-faded shutters and roofs of patched tiles or corrugated iron, steeply pitched to shed the winter snows. The gables of some had once been richly carved but were now so weathered, cracked and split with age that the embellishments were barely visible.

While those houses looked almost as ancient as the oak tree they faced, the buildings around them were drab, Soviet-era constructions, their crumbling concrete façades pockmarked by bullet holes. A huge barn, built of unmilled wood with gaps between the planks, boasted a roof of heavily patched corrugated-iron sheets.

The whole place was mired in mud and poverty. Tangles of scrap metal and rotting timbers decorated the yards. A solitary motor vehicle, a battered Lada with rust-streaked bodywork, was parked next to a pair of horse-drawn farm carts. Apart from a handful of chickens scuttling about and a few cows mooching in the fields, the place seemed to be deserted.

At the side of the road just outside the village, an old door had been nailed to two fence posts driven into the ground. Daubed on it, in crude hand-lettering, was an inscription in Russian, Georgian and Ossetic: 'Protect our village.'

The two men worked their way back from the brow and conferred in low tones. Although his companion was now issuing orders to him, Laszlo's stance and attitude showed that he did not regard him as his superior in any way.

'Ready?' The man's Russian was halting but understandable. And now his accent gave him away.

Laszlo nodded. 'Ready, Englishman.' He signalled to his men and led them down the hill, moving tactically, one foot always on the ground. Half the team stayed where they were to cover the advance of the rest. Using the haystacks to mask their approach, they too went static and returned the favour.

A cock crowed inside a barn and wisps of grey smoke began to rise from a chimney as some unseen inhabitant coaxed his fire into life. Laszlo was wary. It wasn't always like this. An attack could be initiated at any moment. He'd taken incoming from sleepy backwaters like this and lost men. That was why he favoured a rolling start-line. If his team took fire as they approached they'd just roll into the attack and fight their way forward.

They reached the shadows of a tumbledown wall on the edge of the settlement and waited there, all eyes focused on the Englishman as he took one last look at the target to confirm that nothing had changed since he issued his last set of orders the day before.

He'd led them into a field for a run-through in slow time, letting the whole team see what each of the component groups would be doing during the attack. They'd rehearsed the what-ifs: what if the team had a man down? What if a group got separated from the main force? What if the team took heavy fire from an RPG?

Now that the Englishman had seen in real time what he'd told them to call the battle space, he knew there was nothing to add. His voice was calm as he spoke to Laszlo.

The South Ossetian checked that his men were in place and ready, raised his hand, paused a moment, and let it fall.

The team burst from cover. With the Englishman leading one group and Laszlo the other, they advanced along both sides of the main street. Dogs set up a chorus of barks and howls and a few villagers began stumbling from their houses, some clutching hunting rifles and shotguns, one or two with AKs, but the attacking force, better armed and better trained, cut them down before they fired a single round.

Laszlo led his men from house to house. The crump of HE grenades and the crash of splintering wood were interspersed with cries and screams. Half dressed and rubbing sleep from their eyes, the remaining occupants were dragged from their homes, herded into the open, kicked and punched face down into the mud, then immobilized with plastic zip-ties.

While the Englishman stayed with his group and controlled their captives, Laszlo led his team further along the line of buildings. He paused for a couple of seconds, dropped into cover and looked back towards the others. A young villager, perhaps no more than a teenager, was sprinting towards the forest.

Two of the insurgents fired at him and missed. The Englishman dropped to one knee, took careful aim and brought him down with a single shot into the centre of his body mass, then moved forward and finished him with a second to the head.

Laszlo smiled to himself and turned his attention back to the last of the houses. Once it, too, had been searched and cleared, and the occupants secured, the looting began. Food and alcohol were gathered up with as much enthusiasm as the modest treasures the villagers possessed.

Laszlo took a gulp of a fiery local spirit, then passed the bottle among his men. One carried off a fading sepia photograph of a couple dressed for their wedding against a gaudily painted back-drop of a castle. Wanting the ornate frame but not the image it contained, he stamped down with his boot, smashing the glass and ripping the photograph to shreds. He picked out the last shards and propped the frame carefully against the trunk of the oak tree.

Another emerged from an outbuilding clutching a pair of live chickens in each hand. He wrung their necks with practised ease and added them to the growing pile of booty.

On Laszlo's order, the attackers began to separate their male captives from the women, who wailed and keened as husbands and sons were marched and kicked towards the barn at the far edge of the village. Those who resisted were shot where they stood. The rest were herded inside and watched helplessly as its double doors were shut and barred.

Laszlo listened for a moment to the terrified shouts and cries of those trapped within, then nodded to the two men carrying the heavier weapons systems.

They staggered forwards, smashed the windows and directed searing blasts of flame into the barn's interior. Laszlo had selected these weapons with purpose – for the physical pain endured by the dying, and the legacy of mental terror suffered by those unfortunate enough to survive.

In seconds, fuelled by the dry timbers, the hay and straw stored there, the barn was ablaze from end to end. His men stood watch as it burned, and when two villagers somehow succeeded in smashing their way through the disintegrating wall, Laszlo raised his weapon to his shoulder and dropped both targets instantly.

The terrible screams of the remaining victims were soon drowned by the roar of the flames and the crash of falling beams. As the barn collapsed in on itself, the massacre extended even to the villagers' hounds and livestock. The cattle were burned alive with their owners or mown down by gunfire; the dogs were dispatched with a knife thrust or 7.62mm short round.

The flamethrowers now moved among the houses, pausing at each to direct a jet of blazing fluid through the doorway or a shattered window. As they moved on to the next, the one behind them became an inferno. More cries from the women captives were brutally silenced by rifle butts. The attackers showed as little mercy as the Nazis had done in this part of the world just over half a century before.

The SS's *Flammenwerfer*, designed as an infantry weapon to clear out trenches and buildings, had become an instrument of terror when used against civilian populations. It held twelve litres of petrol mixed with tar to make it heavier and increase its range to twenty-five metres. The flaming oil was ignited by a hydrogen torch.

Flammenwerfer operators had been so hated that the trigger and muzzle section of their weapon soon had had to be disguised to look like a standard infantry rifle in an attempt to keep them from being singled out by enemy snipers. Whole villages had been annihilated in its path. Maybe the men here today had had relatives who'd perished in their flames and the pain and fear had been passed down the generations.

Sambor, the more imposing of the operators, was Laszlo's 'little' brother by just thirteen months. He had the same almost lifeless eyes and pallid complexion, but that was where the similarity ended. He had inherited the rest of his physique from his father's family. His massive hands were twice the size of Laszlo's, his fingers like sausages and his hulking frame topped by a riot of dark brown hair, greasy after weeks in the field, which fell to his shoulders.

A child who had somehow escaped detection stumbled out of a nearby building, coughing and choking, smoke streaming from his smouldering hair and clothes. Sambor swung the barrel of his flamethrower back towards the boy and turned him into a human torch. With an unearthly shriek, the blazing figure blundered into a wall before sliding to the ground.

As the dense black column of smoke rose high above the village, Laszlo and two of his men turned their attention to the makeshift sign. Using a piece of scrap iron as a crowbar, they prised the old door away from the posts and pitched it through the window of a blazing house. Within seconds the flames were licking at the painted inscription. The last trace of defiance had now been obliterated, and the centuries-old village erased from the map.

As the ashes swirled around them, the insurgents gathered in the village square, surrounding the captive women. The Englishman had taken as many lives as any, but his expression betrayed nothing of his current thoughts.

Laszlo turned to him. 'You should leave now. Unless . . .' He gestured to the women and gave him a questioning glance. One sat silent, rocking slowly backwards and forwards as her tears carved white streaks through the dirt on her cheeks; others sobbed or pleaded with their stone-faced captors, who were already loosening their belts.

The Englishman shook his head and walked back up the hill towards the waiting trucks. Behind him he could hear a fresh chorus of wavering cries, rising and falling like sirens as the fighters began to take their reward.

Laszlo wouldn't be taking part in what followed. It was a gift from him to his men. Or that was what he had told them. In truth, for Laszlo and the Englishman, this was the final flourish. Just as the flamethrowers spread fear among their potential victims, so did the prospect of rape; and fear, eventually, would bring compliance.

1

London

Pale sunshine bathed the Heath, lighting up the autumn colours of the trees. Nannies clustered on benches, gossiping about their employers while their charges dozed in nearby buggies. A pair of Labradors chased each other in the meadows, deaf to the pleas of their owners, and in the distance a handful of hardy swimmers could be glimpsed braving the bathing pond's frigid waters. Beyond the grand Victorian and Edwardian houses fringing the grassland, the sunlight glinted on the steel and glass towers of the City.

A young couple strolled along a path near the edge of the Heath, arms intertwined, oblivious to everything but each other. Without warning, four black-clad figures burst from the bushes and bundled them swiftly out of sight. Thrown headlong to the ground, the girl arched her back and tried to turn her head as a gloved hand was clamped over her mouth and her wrists were bound with zip-ties. Her eyes widened at the glimpse of matt-black weaponry and the respirator-covered faces of their captors.

The sergeant in command of the fully bombed-up assault team leaned in close. 'Sssh. Stop flapping, hen. You'll not be harmed.' Known as Jockey to his mates, because of his size, and Nasty Bastard to his enemies, he knew his heavy-duty Gorbals accent and the rasp of the respirator's filter were about as comforting as Darth Vader reading a bedtime story, so he tightened his grip and gave it to them straight. 'Both of you – just lie fucking still and keep quiet. Understand?'

They both gave a hesitant nod.

He knelt back on his haunches, hit his pressel switch and spoke quietly into his mic. 'Blue One. Third party secure.'

About Quick Reads

Quick Reads are brilliant short new books written by bestselling writers. They are perfect for regular readers wanting a fast and satisfying read, but they are also ideal for adults who are discovering reading for pleasure for the first time.

Since Quick Reads was founded in 2006, over 4.5 million copies of more than a hundred titles have been sold or distributed. Quick Reads are available in paperback, in ebook and from your local library.

To find out more about Quick Reads titles, visit
www.readingagency.org.uk/quickreads
Tweet us 🐦 @Quick_Reads #GalaxyQuickReads

Quick Reads is part of The Reading Agency,
a national charity that inspires more people to read more, encourages them to share their enjoyment of reading with others and celebrates the difference that reading makes to all our lives.
www.readingagency.org.uk Tweet us @readingagency

The Reading Agency Ltd • Registered number: 3904882 (England & Wales) Registered charity number: 1085443 (England & Wales) Registered Office: Free Word Centre, 60 Farringdon Road, London, EC1R 3GA The Reading Agency is supported using public funding by Arts Council England.

We would like to thank all our funders:

LOTTERY FUNDED

 **has something for everyone**

Stories to make you laugh

Stories to make you feel good

Stories to take you to another place

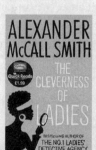

Stories about real life

Stories to take you to another time

Stories to make you turn the pages

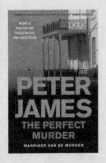

For a complete list of titles visit

www.readingagency.org.uk/quickreads

Available in paperback, ebook and from your local library

Discover the pleasure of reading with Galaxy®

Curled up on the sofa,
Sunday morning in pyjamas,
just before bed,
in the bath or
on the way to work?

Wherever, whenever,
you can escape
with a good book!

So go on...
indulge yourself with
a good read and the
smooth taste of
Galaxy® chocolate.

Proudly supports

Start a new chapter

Too Good To Be True

Ann Cleeves

When young teacher Anna Blackwell is found dead in her home, the police think her death was suicide or a tragic accident. After all, Stonebridge is a quiet village in the Scottish Borders, where murders just don't happen.

But Detective Inspector Jimmy Perez arrives from far-away Shetland when his ex-wife, Sarah, asks him to look into the case. The gossips are saying that her new husband Tom was having an affair with Anna. Could Tom have been involved with her death? Sarah refuses to believe it.

Anna loved kids. Would she kill herself knowing there was nobody to look after her daughter? She had seemed happier than ever before she died. And to Perez, this suggests not suicide, but murder . . .

Start a new chapter

The Double Clue and Other Hercule Poirot Stories

Agatha Christie

Introduced by Sophie Hannah and John Curran

A man is found shot through the head in a locked room.
A wealthy banker disappears while posting a letter. A thief
vanishes with a haul of rubies and emeralds. And, in the
golden sands of Egypt, the men who discovered an
ancient tomb are dying one by one . . .

Hercule Poirot, the fussy Belgian detective with the egg-shaped
head and neat and tidy moustache, solved some of the world's
most puzzling crimes. This book contains four of the very best
stories, selected by John Curran, author of *Agatha Christie's
Secret Notebooks*, and Sophie Hannah, who wrote the brand
new Hercule Poirot novel, *The Monogram Murders*.

Available in paperback, ebook and from your local library

Harper

Why not start a reading group?

If you have enjoyed this book, why not share your next Quick Read with friends, colleagues, or neighbours?

The Reading Agency also runs **Reading Groups for Everyone** which helps you discover and share new books. Find a reading group near you, or register a group you already belong to and get free books and offers from publishers at **readinggroups.org**

A reading group is a great way to get the most out of a book and is easy to arrange. All you need is a group of people, a place to meet and a date and time that works for everyone.

Use the first meeting to decide which book to read first and how the group will operate. Conversation doesn't have to stick rigidly to the book. Here are some suggested themes for discussions:

- How important was the plot?
- What messages are in the book?
- Discuss the characters – were they believable and could you relate to them?
- How important was the setting to the story?
- Are the themes timeless?
- Personal reactions – what did you like or not like about the book?

There is a free toolkit with lots of ideas to help you run a Quick Reads reading group at **www.readingagency.org.uk/quickreads**

Share your experiences of your group on Twitter @Quick_Reads #GalaxyQuickReads

Continuing your reading journey

As well as Quick Reads, The Reading Agency runs lots of programmes to help keep you reading.

Reading Ahead invites you to pick six reads and record your reading in a diary in order to get a certificate. If you're thinking about improving your reading or would like to read more, then this is for you. Find out more at **www.readingahead.org.uk**

World Book Night is an annual celebration of reading and books on 23 April, which sees passionate volunteers give out books in their communities to share their love of reading. Find out more at **worldbooknight.org**

Reading together with a child will help them to develop a lifelong love of reading. Our **Chatterbooks** children's reading groups and **Summer Reading Challenge** inspire children to read more and share the books they love. Find out more at **readingagency.org.uk/children**

Find more books for new readers at

- **www.readingahead.org.uk/find-a-read**
- **www.newisland.ie**
- **www.barringtonstoke.co.uk**